Achievement

Joyce Lange Cowen

Achievement

A Short Story

by

Joyce Lange Cowen

Published by Nenge Books, Australia, September 2023
ABN 26809396184
nengebooks1@gmail.cpm
www.nengebooks.com

Layout and desktop by Nenge Books

Story and artwork © 2023 Joyce Lange Cowen

Cover picture - Adobe Stock #218177663

(Also available as an ebook: ISBN 978-0-6456758-0-1)

ISBN 978-0-6456758-9-4

Dedication

This story is dedicated to many of the girls who worked on dairy farms throughout 1930-1950 and who could not fulfill their aspirations. Some left the farms, but many had to stay – the Second World War was taking so many of their brothers far away to keep the enemy at bay.

Those who escaped the daily grind of the dairy worked in the local towns as waitresses, sales-girls, or in the telephone exchange. Some studied music, dress and pattern making. Some though continued their education at the high school – they were the lucky ones. They were able to work as bank assistants, clerks, book-keepers and receptionists.

In this story, Janine longed to be referred to as an office girl, thus leaving the farm girl image behind her.

Contents

Acknowledgements

I would like to acknowledge the invaluable assistance of my daughters Julie Cason and Ruth Eddy and my friend Dulcie Reeves.

Prologue

Janine worked on a dairy farm with her dad, as her brothers had enlisted in the army in the Second World War. Young women like her usually had a boyfriend, married at a young age and continued working on the farms close by. Before her mum had passed away a few years previously, she had suggested Byron as a boyfriend and hoped Janine would marry him one day. Janine, however, had aspirations of further education and wanted to leave the farm.

In 1945 the atomic bomb had been dropped on Hiroshima and an Armistice declared; WWII was over. Janine's brothers returned home unscathed and would continue running the farm, as her father wanted to retire. Money was scarce, butter only brought sixpence per pound to the farmers.

Janine could now leave to live in Murwillumbah and follow her dreams; she would find work and save money so she could train for office work.

She packed up her frugal belongings, said goodbye to her father and brothers and her farm pets, and rode her push bike three miles to the Kunghur Post Office where she loaded her push bike onto, then boarded, the Kyogle to Murwillumbah bus and began her dream.

In Murwillumbah she found a tiny two roomed flat then went to see the proprietor of the Austral Café, who employed her to start the following week.

Her boyfriend, Byron, was happy for her, although he did not understand how high she was aiming – marriage was not first on her list of priorities – she had this crazy notion of getting more education!!

Janine's school horse
Swaggy

1. Dairy Farm Girl

Marriage is not for me, well, maybe later, but not yet. It's what everyone expects of farm girls, isn't it? Byron hasn't exactly asked me, however everything he says points to marriage between us. I just feel that I would like to do one thing to please myself. No, I am not self-centred but I think there's more to life than just being a wife and mother. I love the farm life but I desperately want to break out from the expectations and make something else of my life now.

I'd found myself work at George's local cafe and thought perhaps I could study at home in my tiny rented flat in town on my days off. Finally having study time would be the essence. George, my boss, is a most understanding guy, so I decided to discuss my ideas with him.

Many people decide to study counselling, but no, that's not for me, counselling is taking on other people's problems – no! Different occupations come to mind, then suddenly accountancy pops into my head, I've heard that the pay is good, that's if everyone pays their accounts! I realize that maths is not my forte, however accountancy would help me to learn more about it. I may even become a maths whiz - just joking!

The more I think about it the more I realize that it would be the kind of challenge that's exactly what I need. I am tired of being referred to as 'the little girl from the dairy farm'. Yes, I will study accountancy. If I can't handle the work, I'll study something else. The saying goes, 'If I tried and failed at least I've proved to myself that I had a go'. I need to do this just to prove that I can. I'm not egoistic, I just feel there is more to life for me then just being a waitress.

George is such an understanding guy. Because of my health he allows me to take a morning off sometimes when necessary. After telling him of my aspirations, he looks at me and says, "I could tell that there's more to you than meets the eye. Your thoughts are not always on your work; no, they are not romantic thoughts - that guy of yours is the unluckiest man, he seems to care a lot for you so please let him down gently. You need to give more thought to what you intend to study, however I will back you all the way." I give George an excited kiss on his cheek and hurry off.

My thoughts about finding time for studying weigh heavily on my mind. I am a full-time waitress, finding time to study will be hard although George did say he would back me all the way. I could possibly fit in study time on those mornings when I can't go to work, and at weekends too.

Byron will not be happy; however, he is not my first priority. I will ease out of my relationship with him, spend less time with him. He may not like what I'm doing, however he is very involved in sport; cricket all summer and tennis, which takes up many of his winter weekends. I may encourage him to attend fitness classes where he may find someone else to fill in time with. Yes, I think I'll encourage him to enrol - it will also improve his physique.

There is a young guy, John, who does my dad's accounts. My dad admires him greatly, I think I'll make an appointment with him and have a chat. If he's not very encouraging? …..well! Here goes, I'll dial his number now – perhaps he can take me on as a trainee?

John arranges for us to meet the very next day. I enlighten him about my weakness in maths and he says I would be a challenge he's willing to take on.

After the interview I feel a little light-headed. As I leave John's office my feet don't seem to engage with terra firma: I am soon to embark on a new adventure, I never thought any of this would ever happen to me! I always dreamed of something more fulfilling than being a waitress.

2. Setting Priorities

With all arrangements underway, now I need to tell Byron of my aspirations. We'll go for a walk in the park, which I arrange for Sunday. We will eat our lunch in the park. I'll prepare something scrumptious plus his favourite, a sponge cake, which my mum Connie taught me how to cook - she was a marvellous cook.

Byron is very quiet but he did compliment me for the cake; we both enjoy it with thick whipped cream and strawberry jam. I now have to break the news to Byron. When I finish telling him of my impending studies, he asks,

"Where do I fit in?"

"Well, you are a sports freak," I reply, "I don't fit in with your plans. You will have more time with your cricket mates. You won't have to worry about leaving them early and finding a ride to my place. You will be able to go home earlier and get more sleep and be refreshed to spend time with me after church and not go to sleep as you usually do."

He was quiet but I am excited, which Byron notices. I am about to plunge into an exciting new adventure.

"Maybe I'll just pop in to see you through the week sometimes." says Byron. "I thought we had a good thing going which would lead us to being happily together ever after."

I do not look exactly approving - we are not engaged to be married, no promises have been made to each other, so why do I feel guilty? We kiss good bye, Byron walks away.

I tell George everything, he is happy for me.

"I wish you the best, hope it all works out for you." he says.

That was more than Byron said, but Byron seems to be only thinking of what Byron wants and didn't give me a thought. As George departs, he says jokingly,

"Now dairy girl, don't take too many sick days."

I thank him with a kiss on the cheek and merrily go back to my tiny unit to set about making room to study.

My thoughts are still on Byron's reaction and what else I can do to distract him from me. Then my friend Colleen comes to mind… oh yes, a plan begins to form in my mind. Most people who know her know that she is in love with Byron. I will invite her to have a meal here on Saturday evening. She and Byron will make a great pair, and both are Christians. Colleen is healthier, stronger than I and she would fit in with Byron's plans for sure.

Colleen accepts my invitation and agrees to be here by 6pm. Byron will arrive around the same time: wonderful, everything is going according to plan!

My kitchen is tiny, three rooms rolled into one, and the seating is ideal to suit my plan. Colleen arrives first and sits on the corner seat that wraps around my kitchen table - you know, the sort that is in restaurants. I pour her a cool drink and she becomes very chatty, asking me about my work at the café. I pretend to really enjoy it, but also say that it's not long-term work, meaning that I want to improve myself, to increase my knowledge.

She looks at me quizzically and says, "So you don't see marriage in your near future?"

"That will be much later." I reply, "No, Byron and I have not planned anything together, we are just coasting along. I am still very young and have heaps of time for marriage and children, there is more to life right now."

Byron arrives and is surprised to find Colleen at my place.

"I've invited an old friend now that I have a place of my own," I greet him with. "I thought we could get together sometimes and maybe play Scrabble."

"Good idea," says Colleen. "Hello Byron, great to see you, it's been ages."

She moves along the seat and pats the seat beside her.

"Sit here Byron, there's plenty of room."

He sits near her and looks a little bit uncomfortable; she doesn't notice and directs her conversation to Byron. This pleases me, as I need to concentrate on the preparation of the meal.

As she chats to Byron, she moves a little closer to him. I smile; plans are moving forward. She and Byron become engrossed in his cricket game scores; he has helped his team win the match by clean bowling the opposing team's best batsman, he is in high spirits.

I serve him his favourite drink and their conversation continues as Colleen moves even closer to Byron. There is nowhere to move away, he is on the end of the seat. They sit very close now and she touches his hand; they look so cosy. Her nearness doesn't seem to affect him, he has no romantic feeling for her at all.

The meal goes well, Colleen even compliments me about my cooking and presentation, she is in high spirits all night. Byron becomes quiet and when I congratulate him on winning the game, he barely acknowledges my flattery.

Not long after the meal Byron excuses himself, says he has had a hectic day and needs to go early. I pretend disappointment and suggest he could drop Colleen off at her place. "Yes, okay," he replies curtly. I watch them drive away together and am pleased my plan might work. But I don't want to count my chickens before they hatch.

My life continues on the same as usual and I really start to enjoy my work as many old school friends come into the Austral Cafe. I remember my family enjoying eating out here even though we could only afford the cheapest meal, such as pie, peas and potato plus gravy. It was great for mum, no cooking or dishes to wash, it was the highlight of her week.

3. A New Beginning

On Monday 5th August I awake excited. I start my training with John. Excitement grows, how will I handle my first day? I know John will not expect too much from me. We had a few chats through the week and he even came over to the restaurant for a meal twice last week. George gave me a few minutes off work while John and I became more acquainted, settling my fears just in case he may expect too much from me. No, he was very polite and I feel more at ease.

In no time my first day is over. I feel calm and the homework John gave me to do looks quite easy, I feel I can handle it and it proves to be no trouble at all.

The days pass and the homework, which I manage very well, continues. However I know that the hard stuff is to come, John is just testing my ability, finding out how much I do know about mathematics.

Byron comes as usual after cricket on Saturday. The season will finish soon, he has had another good game and is jubilant about his efforts, he bowled four overs and the opposing team lost four batsmen.

Yes, Byron loves the game of cricket. At the end of the season trophies will be presented. I don't really understand the game and am not interested in sport at all. No, I am not the one for Byron and I'm sure Colleen knows that.

After we eat, I ask if he delivered Colleen safely to her doorstep.

"Yes" he replies simply.

When I ask if he has seen her around, he says, "No, she doesn't move in my circles."

On Sunday Colleen turns up at the same church that Byron and I attend. She sits towards the back and invites Byron to sit beside her. I am out of sight over near the vestry door and toward the front row and watch what happens. Yes, this pleases me a lot, Colleen has waited for him to arrive.

The Church lesson is about care for others and forgetting self. Well, isn't that what I am doing? Trying to please Colleen. She is infatuated with Byron and he will make her such a good husband. They both come back to my place and I rustle up some lunch, mainly egg and lettuce sandwiches - I apologise to be only serving sandwiches! Both thank me.

I have chores to do this afternoon, so I ask if they would mind leaving me so I can get them done. As well, George needs me to come to work. One of the other girls has taken time off as her mother is ill and I am needed to help in the kitchen. More money in my pay packet, for which I am pleased.

Byron's visits become more infrequent. I never know if he will visit on Saturday evenings or not. I have a phone connected so there is no excuse for him not to call, but he just pops in unannounced at any old time, usually around mealtime. This doesn't worry me as George always sends me home with leftovers; usually heaps of roast beef, chicken or lamb.

My homework becomes more intense, so I need more time to complete it. Byron visits less and less as I do not have time for him. I miss him but my life has changed, I have become a study freak.

One day as I sit leisurely reading 'The Daily Mail' newspaper I see there is a picture of Byron receiving his cricket awards. Right there in the front seat is Colleen, clapping her hands. Wow, this is just what I wanted. Byron is wearing an ear-to-ear smile, my does he look happy!

The very next Saturday Byron visits me, no phone call, just a leisurely walk in.

"Anyone home?" he calls. I put my pen down and meet him at my bedroom door, just like old times. I am a little annoyed, from now on I will lock the screen door day and night. As I make him a pot of tea, I pretend I am glad to see him and even give him a kiss.

Actually, I am glad to see him, some of the old feelings of affection are still there. I congratulate him on his cricket awards.

"Did you see the picture and who was with me?" he asks.

"Yes," I reply, making no other comment. He shares that he and Colleen are now an item, she is so interested in cricket and accompanies him to the match every Saturday. I try not to look too upset, or too happy for them, however a little bit of jealousy shows its evil head. What am I doing, this is what I wanted? Why this guilty, jealous reaction?

Byron holds me in his arms - I don't resist. I accept his kiss then guiltily push him away.

"No, we musn't do this anymore, you belong to Colleen now, I will not trespass on her ground, I am happy for you both," I tell him.

"So we are finished then?" Byron asks. I nod in agreement and he finishes his cuppa and leaves. I really think Byron expects me to reverse my decision about him, I mean he is a good-looking sportsman, and I am a little jealous. Too bad, we are finished now, I must continue with John and my new venture.

The lessons are going well. So far nothing I can't handle, however I know the hard part is ahead of me. Life continues on and I succeed in fitting everything in, a little surprised when I don't need to take many mornings off work. Seems it was Byron who really took up much of my time in the past.

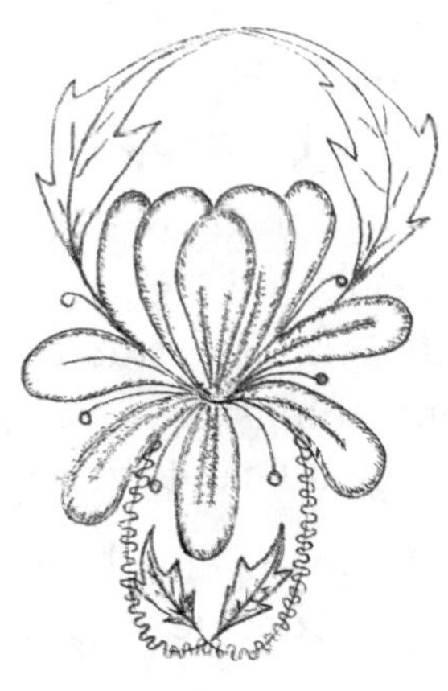

4. A New Romance

I always look at the headlines, then the births, marriages, engagements when reading our local newspaper and so some time later I am shocked when I pick up the paper and a picture of Byron and Colleen peers out at me, announcing their engagement. Phew that is quick, it's only six months ago he was kissing me! Oh well, they are both older than me by five years - it's really goodbye Byron now.

I hurry early to work on Monday, I need to buy an engagement card. I find a really lovely one and post it to Byron's address.

My work is much the same, waitressing doesn't change, only perhaps we are busier on this Thursday - pension day. I am run off my feet and George notices I have to have a rest after lunch. He comes over and suggests I head home. I gratefully accept.

The next morning, I take a sickie. George has been expecting me to call, and I go back to bed and sleep right through till 2pm. The studies and work are too much for me and things have caught up with me. I think I'll ask George if I can have a week off.

There is a bus trip up to O'Reilly's in the ranges inland from the Gold Coast. I decide to go, and have a complete change of scenery. When I return, I feel wonderful. There is a note pinned to my door, from Byron. It says, 'I just wanted to see you once more before I marry Colleen, love Byron.'

They marry a few weeks after his visit. I hope and pray for their happiness.

A whole year has passed since I started studying with John, who is pleased with my progress. Of course, the studies are harder and I struggled at times. Those are the times when John spends time sorting me out. We have such a great rapport with each other that he offers me a partnership and will form a company with me. Well, that is in the future, a few years to go yet or maybe not?

At times the studies become too hard and I suggest to John that I can't go on. I don't seem to be getting anywhere. His reply is, "Take a break, have a week off," which I happily take. George notices and doesn't work me too hard.

There is another announcement in the paper. I read them all but this one is special. 'Mr. and Mrs. Byron and Colleen Gowers' son was born 8 pounds 14oz, named Bevan Arthur.' Wow, that is a large first baby! I'm sure the old people, Byron's parents, will be pleased. I had trouble visualising a smile on Byron's Mum's face because she mainly only scowled at me. That's why Byron didn't take me to visit them after the first two visits, he could see their dislike of me.

I've sent a baby boy card, a really sentimental, special one. I hope I didn't overdo the congrats, and hope it makes them happy.

This is my last year of studies and my, do I swat and swat. I try to memorize so much. Maths is going round and round in my head but you know what? I actually get it; can't imagine why I thought maths was so hard.

John notices the difference in me, he can see my elation and buzzes me into his office.

"Today, girl, is the turning point in your life. You can give up your waitressing job and become a fully-fledged accountant."

I sit there in shock; I was not expecting this. I have passed all my exams; John has got me through the accountancy course in three years. No wonder I feel drained but jubilant all at the same time.

I kiss John, we laugh together and I even pull him out of his chair and waltz him around his office. Suddenly I realize just what I have done because John is holding me a little too tight and suddenly kisses me hard on my lips. I pull away from him, my face turns red and John realizes what he has done. His face turns the same colour as mine and he sort of trips into his chair, apologizing as he crashes. I sit down rather quietly, out of breath, and don't know where to look or what to do, then I solemnly say to John, "I'm sorry, how stupid of me, I just became too excited, not like me at all."

As I get up to leave, John says, "No Janine, I shouldn't have kissed you like that, I just got caught up in the moment. Perhaps you need to leave now, I'll be in touch, I'll give you a call."

I walk home, even forgetting my push bike, make tea and sit down, not sure what has just occurred. My mind is in shock, the whole of me is very shaken, I don't quite understand just what has happened. I drink my tea, take an aspirin and go to bed.

When next morning arrives, confusion about the kiss remains. I decide to go to work at the cafe, it will give me something else to think about. George detects my woeful face and later asks me about my morbid expression. He expected to see me looking very elated, he knew I was expecting to have a good report when I saw John.

"What's the matter, girl? You look as though you got bad results, as though you didn't pass your exams," he asks.

No, I will not discuss the kiss with George, it is too personal. John and George are friends, I need to keep this to myself.

"Yes, I passed and have been offered a partnership by John. I'm so grateful to him, he has really changed my life. I don't feel like a hillbilly anymore. I wish my parents were here to know how happy and educated I've become."

"You don't look overly excited, what's up?" George asks.

I just say, "I was feeling a little down, overly excited and now I've just slumped, think I'll go home."

George agrees.

Soon after getting home the phone rings and it is John. He wants to see me and asks me to come over. I've had a rest and feel much more like myself. I casually greet him and he sits down looking a little anxious.

I say, "John don't worry, I know you got caught up in the moment, we were both so excited. I'm sorry. Let's go back to where we were before that little episode."

The anxiety leaves John's face and he relaxes.

"I'm so glad you are so forgiving, that's exactly what it was all about, please forgive me?"

We shake hands as I thank him for all he has done for me and put the jug on. We have a leisurely cuppa.

"Are you OK to start work on Monday?" John asks me. This was Wednesday.

"Yes, see you then," I reply.

5. A New Boy in my Life

Would you believe Byron turns up saying that Colleen isn't very well? I wonder why he is telling me; we hadn't seen each other for ages. He says that after their baby boy was born, she never recovered to her normal self and is now pregnant again and in a lot of abdominal pain. Why is he telling ME all this? He seems very distressed. Well, I make another pot of tea and sit down to listen.

His next utterance is to ask me if I would mind his little boy, Bevan, for tomorrow. This is a surprise. "Colleen's so ill she isn't coping, please," he pleads.

Why me? I wondered, "Where's the family?" I ask.

"They have all moved away from the area, gone to work and live near a mining town in Queensland. There is just no one I can ask and I wouldn't let my little boy be cared for by anyone I didn't know," Byron replies.

Well, this is the last straw!

"Look Byron, I've a hectic week, bring Bevan over this afternoon, bring his favourite toys and we will become acquainted before tomorrow; you stay here too, just a couple of hours." He agrees to my suggestion, not asking me how my health is or about my studies, he still can't think beyond what he wants or needs.

Bevan is still a baby not yet two years old; he seems a well-adjusted child and not shy at all, very much like Colleen. He sits on the floor and plays with his toys. He looks up and smiles at both of us and drinks the contents of his bottle. Byron has to get Bevan's clothes from the ute. The little boy watches for his return, he doesn't become agitated at all and smiles at me. There is an ache in my heart, he could have been mine. Just goes to show that I had never gotten over the love affair, I was so sure I had.

"I see you are both getting along well, I am sure he won't be any trouble," says Byron.

The next day Bevan settles in well. I must say I enjoy the day with him. Colleen comes that afternoon to collect her boy, she really looks pallid and very thin, she thanks me.

"The specialist recommended that I have my gall bladder removed, the x-rays indicated that it is diseased," she tells me, explaining her illness.

She then asks if she can count on me to mind her boy again, maybe for a few days? She will need someone whom Byron can depend on.

"When, how soon?" I enquire.

"Next weekend," she replies. "Next weekend, surgery is on Monday."

I check with George and John and both give me time off, although John had agreed to give me a month's holiday before starting work in his office. I have been fill in waitressing for George when he is up to his eyeballs with work; after all, I have been his head waitress and am always willing to fill in now when needed. He always gives me the leftovers, so I need not cook after work.

Bevan comes for the day and we have the greatest time together, what a darling little boy he is, I hold him close to me, I am enjoying every minute.

Colleen's surgery goes well; however, she miscarries her second little baby boy. Byron keeps in touch with me by phone and collects Bevan two days later; he says he will care for him over the weekend. He is rather solemn and says that Colleen is very sick and is being kept in hospital for now. It may be another week until she will be able to return home.

"If you need me, you know where I live," I offer Byron. He nods and goes on his merry way. Well, not too merry, he looks rather grim. Colleen is not doing well and he knows it.

Bevan plays around here on the Monday as though it is his home; well it is his second home now. He comes to stay often through the next week, luckily I am still on my month of holiday. I really look forward to his daily visits, he is so very good, only cries when he is tired and I know to fill his bottle and to put him to bed. He sleeps two hours each day so I have time to go over my studies.

John pops around with some work for me to do, he says he really needs me to start work soon. Well, another week passes and Bevan is dropped off yet again. I inform Byron that the following week I have to go to the office and begin my new job.

"I realize that," he says. "I'm not sure if Colleen can cope, she is still in pain, I don't think the surgery was successful, I'm taking her back to the specialist tomorrow."

In the meantime, George is preparing a small party for me. He phones and says, "Would you be free tomorrow? I would like you to come to the cafe around eleven o'clock."

Tomorrow is Saturday and I answer, "Yes, tomorrow will be fine."

Little do I know that Colleen is back in hospital and Bevan will be left with me. Byron is so distressed that he forgets about him and when he phones around 6pm on Friday, he is so very upset.

"I'm staying at the hospital tonight, Colleen is back here in Lismore Base and may need to have surgery again," he informs me.

"Okay Byron," I answer, "yes, he's good." Before I can ask him about tomorrow, he hangs up. Well, I understand how worried he must be about his wife but he's taking me for granted. Sure, I will mind the little boy but I will have to take him with me tomorrow to George's Cafe. Byron forgot about asking me if I have plans. Oh well, Bevan needs to come with me.

I phone George and inform him of my situation. "Well there's nothing else for you to do but bring him with you, I'll send a taxi to bring you both to the café," he says.

I pack up some toys, make up a bottle and tie him into the cloth baby carrier, strap it around my waist and tie the shoulder strap. He is a smallish child, if he wasn't he would have had to walk beside me - when I take Bevan outside, he usually runs off. I dislike the halter and strap; it reminds me of taking the dog for a walk. This little boy has become very precious to me.

The taxi arrives and the drive is a short trip to the café; we are driven to the door and to my surprise a sign hangs right across the doorway, "Congratulations Janine". I am taken by surprise, flabbergasted! My waitressing friends, John and George all cheer, clap and call out, "surprise, surprise." I am very surprised; most give me a hug and John presents the award I have earned.

Bevan smiles and claps too. Most of the girls think that he is my baby because I haven't worked at the café full time in the past few years. They soon find out he is Byron's baby once I explain the situation. The certificate all framed and presented to me prove to the girls just where I have been and what I have achieved in those three short years.

I put Bevan down, he is soon having a great time with one of my friends. The girls love him. "I don't deserve all this," I say to George and John.

"Oh yes you do, you have been juggling two jobs and these past two weeks, have looked after a baby boy. We can't imagine how you have coped so you know what we are going to do for you?" said John, "We are giving you another month off, you don't have to start at the office until next month." Surprise and delight fill my face.

Both men make speeches and enlighten all about my studies while trying to work at the cafe to support myself, noting that just when I gained my Diploma of Accountancy I was asked to care for a little boy. There is more clapping and congratulations by everyone. I am then given a cake to cut, then tea, cake, coffee and a smorgasbord of food is devoured. I feel a little lightheaded and sit down, all this celebrating is too much, however I appreciate it and joyfully close my eyes briefly and say, 'Thank you Lord'.

George arranges to have a taxi take Bevan and I home. I am so tired I have to lie down. Bevan joins me and we sleep together on my bed. I am awakened by a loud noise, someone banging on the back door. Bevan doesn't wake up so I creep out to find his dad waiting to enter. I let him in. He looks tired and says,

"Where were you, you look as though you were sleeping?"

"I was, Bevan is still asleep, we had a party this morning."

"Whose party?" asks Byron.

"Well, as I mentioned to you the party was for me. I was presented with my award, there's my certificate framed over there on the bench. I guess I will hang it somewhere tomorrow."

"Oh," he said, "congratulations." Then he went on to say that he too needs sleep, he has been with his wife for two days and three nights at the hospital.

I ask, "How is she?"

"Not good at all, we may lose her."

I am not expecting that answer. "I will keep Bevan until tomorrow if you like while you go home and sleep." He looks thankful and hurries off.

I can't be sure how long Bevan will be with me but I can't toss him out into the street can I? I love this little boy. He wakes saying, 'daddy' 'daddy', he must have dreamed about his Dad. I pacify him with food and his bottle, we have a little chat and soon it is bedtime again. No sign of Byron, "Oh well, his visits are erratic," I say aloud, I do understand, especially at this time.

6. Tragedy

Two more days pass - it is now Wednesday and finally Byron turns up, I put the jug on and let him in. I haven't had breakfast and Bevan slept late. Byron looks like something the cat has dragged in. I can't help but put my arms around him to give him comfort. I sit him at the table as he weeps. He eventually tells me that Colleen has passed away. I bring his tea and toast over to him and sit close as I drink mine; he eventually calms himself and begins to eat what I have prepared for him. I feel devasted for him.

Colleen had become unconscious and never woken up, she slipped away at about 5am this morning, he was by her side, and he has forgotten to eat since early yesterday.

"Did you drive yourself home?"

"No, someone put me on a bus and it let me off at the corner near home," Byron stammers. He had then walked over here. I guess the fresh air helped keep him awake. I suggest he lays on my bed near his son, which he eagerly agrees to. He is so exhausted and looks absolutely gutted.

A little later I peep into the bedroom and see both Byron and Bevan are fast asleep. I quietly pick up my studies and escape to the kitchen. Thoughts of Colleen pervade my mind, she was a friend but now she has gone to glory. It is too much to believe and I weep for the little boy she has left behind and for Byron who is completely devastated. She will be sadly missed for a long time.

Finally, Byron awakes when his son becomes noisy, jumping up and down on the bed. He carries Bevan into the kitchen and says, "Well best we go home."

"I've put enough dinner on to cook for all of us, please stay," I urge him. He does stay but leaves soon after dinner.

Next day I make up my mind to go away for a few days, after all, Byron has his parents, surely, they would mind Bevan. I let George know then catch a bus to Queensland. Not sure where I am going, I need a rest, a whole week would be great. So I book into a motel so I don't have to cook, all meals are provided. I can sleep in as long as I want. Only George knows where I am.

One day Byron calls him to ask where I have gone. George tells him that I have gone away to have a complete rest. Byron is very upset.

"Why now?" he says to George, "She knows that I need her."

George cannot help himself, saying, "Always thinking of yourself and your needs." He walks away, leaving Byron standing there.

Arriving home, I find a note from Byron pinned to my door. After reading it I feel very upset. It says, 'You walked out on us, I never expected you to leave us in the lurch. ' Byron thinking always about himself, same Byron, no change.

Feeling refreshed, after my break, I phone John and say, "Could you use me and my expertise this week?"

John is surprised. "Yes, yes, pleased to hear from you, come in if you want to."

I pack my new briefcase, which is a gift from all those at my party, and ride my push bike into the office. It is good to be here. John greets me pleasantly.

"I have something to show you." He opens a door beside his office and says, "This is all yours." I am elated to see the office he has prepared all for me.

"Sit down and try the chair, cast your eyes around the room. I'll bring you morning tea."

It is all too much; the excitement is overpowering and I sit there dazed. John returns with a tray and sits down at my desk.

"What's the matter cowgirl, where are your thoughts? I hoped you would be thrilled."

I am jolted back to earth.

"You are not meaning me because I am an Accountant, look what this plaque says," I refute. John has even had my name and status printed on the door plaque, and it is ready to be attached to my door. Just then George enters. I did wonder why there were three cups. The men make a little ceremony over attaching the plaque, both kiss me and we three sit down to eat and celebrate.

I show George the note Byron left on my door.

"After all that you have done for him, looked after his little boy and even fed Byron as well, what a guy he is. Why don't you marry me?" asks George. I take his offer as a joke and laugh it off.

When George leaves John tells me, "You know George is serious about you, his offer was not a joke, you need to talk to him."

I spend the whole week in my office. I am thrilled, my spirits leap high. Do I really have my Accountancy Diploma? But I need to think about George's proposal.

So I phone George and ask him to come over if he has time on Saturday, and we will try to sort out what is happening.

He comes on time and soon we are in discussion. George is serious, "You know that I'm in love with you, don't you?" he tells me.

I am very surprised. "No. I really admire you and am thankful for all your help. I just thought you cared about me trying to improve myself." How can I tell him the truth honestly?

"I'm sorry George, I don't want to marry anyone. I need to prove myself now and become a fully-fledged Accountant with at least twelve months experience under my belt."

George tries to smile and says, "Don't let my proposal worry you, I'll wait for you." Looks as though I'll have to do some more match making and find someone for George!

7. Breaking Down Stereotypes

Life continues on for me, work is interesting. There are clients who are a little anxious that a girl is doing their accounts. John decides to check all my work in front of the client. I don't mind at all so long as the client is happy.

I decide to ask John to accept the work from clients who question my reliability and I will stay in my office. John says that my certificates are on the wall for clients to see and the difficult ones can go elsewhere if they don't trust my ability.

Would you believe that I find a few more areas in the client's tax returns where deductions can be claimed, ones that John has missed - new places are appearing for the clients to claim and they are tax deductible. This really pleases the 'hard to get along with' old guy. He comes in to congratulate me one day, says that his tax is much lower than the year before.

When the old codger leaves, I stand up and clap, John does also, we laugh together and decide to take a break. That old guy has a complete turnaround that pleases both of us.

George asks me to help at the cafe occasionally. We stay good friends. He doesn't speak to me again about romance, for which I am relieved.

Late one Saturday afternoon there is a knock on my door. I have been doing an account for the happy old guy and I have to get it right. I am being especially scrupulous. I have to be precise, and now I have to drop everything to answer the door.

There stands Byron with Bevan. I am surprised to say the least, Byron has not been in touch with me since he left that horrible note, nor has he been at church. I let them in and put a happy smile on my face. Bevan has forgotten me; however, Byron kisses me just like old times and says, "I missed you."

"Me too" I reply, and invite them to come in. Bevan climbs up on the wraparound seat and Byron follows. I put the kettle on and prepare a cuppa, I especially need one.

"Did you play cricket today, Byron?" I ask him.

"No I haven't played this season," he replies. "Bevan needs to be taken care of. Mum can only do a certain amount. Bevan runs her ragged. I even have to take Bevan to work with me. On the weekends I am busy with the washing and the house needs cleaning."

Bevan must be over two years old by now? A little voice chirps up, "I am two and a half, I'm a big boy now, mummy."

Bevan does remember me after all, my heart misses a beat, then Bevan adds, "I would like a drink please."

Byron watches as a smile crosses my face and my eyes brighten up, he is pleased with the results as its clear that Bevan does remember me.

"You will stay for dinner then?"

Byron answers in the affirmative.

I ask Byron if the sadness of his loss is lessening.

"Just a little," he says, "Colleen was such a good mate, always put her needs on the back burner, she loved to accompany me to every cricket match and was excited when I had a win. I used to hear her and Bevan clapping and hear them say 'good one daddy'. Yes, I miss those times. She was a good housewife too, everything in its place, she also made all Bevan's clothes and loved him so much." Tears threaten and his voice breaks a little. Bevan leans over and kisses his dad and I fill up a little too.

"This I knew, Colleen would make you happy and be a good wife, she loved you Byron," I say as we compose ourselves and continue on with our conversation.

He continued, "I don't understand why she had to die so young, yes, far too young."

Byron thanks me for dinner and Bevan gives me a cuddle and says, "Bye Mummy". Byron gives me an unusual smile as they depart.

My life continues on, no waves of disagreement, all work-related emotions under control, and my health improves. I have achieved my goal and intend to work hard for John. He is very good to me. I can work at the office or at home, I do enjoy my lifestyle.

John becomes engaged, his fiancée is a lovely young woman. He met Lucille on a cruise. Both were looking for romance and found each other. There is a party organized for next week and I am invited, it will be a dress up affair.

John explains to me, "Janine, I want you to buy the prettiest dress you can find, don't worry about the cost I'll help pay for it. Please, I want my business partner to be well dressed and looking her very best."

To find something flashy I need to go to the Gold Coast. I ask Flora to go with me for a second opinion, I need her as she is a fancy dresser and she is about the only female friend with whom I have kept in touch, and she is invited to the party as well.

The party is in full swing when Flora and I arrive. We are both wearing very expensive frocks and are in party mood. We intend letting our hair down and having a whooping time. Now that expression does not sound like the professional woman I have become, sounds more like the old dairy maid I was! I must control my emotions and become more sophisticated.

John greets Flora and I, and whistles; the dress is working miracles plus the makeup and hair - the beautician has performed miracles.

Flora and I enjoy the party. "We will have to start kicking our heels up from now on." I say to her.

"Yes," says Flora, "This is fun." We do not drink alcohol even through there is plenty there.

Next day is Saturday and I sleep in till ten, I feel so relaxed, life is good. However, I must get out of this dump where I live, my clothes have to be washed outside, rain, hail or shine. Cut wood is delivered to me so I can boil the copper and washing has to be done often. You may not believe it, but I only have two changes of work clothes and about four other outfits.

John had also said, "You need some very smart suits to liven up that clever girl image in the office and don't forget the high heels, you don't know how gorgeous you looked at the party."

I told him, "Flattery will get you nowhere."

I take John's advice and when Lucille visits one day she comments to John, "Is that the same girl you showed me the photo of when we were on the cruise? I'll have to keep a watchful eye on you two."

8. The Test of Time

Byron has now become a regular visitor, bringing Bevan with him always. I really didn't have the heart to turn them away and now I look forward to their visits. Byron has changed, he adores his son and even gave up sport to keep the little guy happy. Byron is a changed man and it shows - my love for him has never changed. Sometimes he puts his arm around me and kisses me either hello or goodbye. I don't react - it is much too soon, Colleen only left this world about eight months ago and, when I remind Byron of this, he smiles and says, "I know."

Work is wonderful, I make good money and am saving for a car. The move into a nice unit goes smoothly, Byron helps out with his ute, which makes the move so much easier for me. I love this little unit, it even has a sitting room for entertaining my friends and it is cosy, a thick carpet on the floor adds to my comfort. This is where my friends and I can sit to play Scrabble and Mah-jong in enjoyable surroundings.

I begin to invite some of my church friends around as well, there is a need in my life for more company and companionship. In the past my whole life of study and work depleted me of many friends and of course the tiny unit was not a decent place to entertain anyone. I hope to keep working for a few more years before settling down to become a house wife and mother.

Byron calls every few weeks and to keep him from becoming too serious with me I invite friends over. At least two pop in for dinner as they know when Byron chooses to visit. His overt attention toward me has to be kept at bay, so Flora always stays, being the last to leave. She knows that I don't want to be alone with Byron. He always kisses me goodnight and I really want his intentions for me to stop there.

It is time to look for a car, my old bike is worn out. I will buy a new car and I hope it will serve me well, a second-hand car may break down and in the long run cost me more for repairs. Hope I am not biting off more than I can chew but that little maroon Holden is so very beautiful. I throw caution to the wind and buy it. This beauty will take me anywhere, and will deliver me to the farm lands, rain, hail or shine. Then I make my first payment.

My excitement grows. John can see my wide smile as I report to him about my new possession. "You haven't even got a drivers licence yet!"

"I'll get onto that this weekend, I have a permit, so I'm ready to go. Byron has promised to take me out into the country for starters, you know he even helped me to move house."

"My goodness I thought he was past tense," said John.

"I did too, but he has popped up again. Thank you for giving me time off to move."

I kiss him for his goodness to me but he has to be pushed away. John sort of holds me a little more tightly than required but the smile does not waver. He knows that I want to be my own woman and I have every intention of working for a few years before marriage will control my life. I will become a well-established Accountant.

Byron keeps up his pursuit of me. I work long hours in the office, but he still calls in on a Saturday evening and he and Bevan have dinner with me. He usually comes to church and I teach Bevan in a Sunday school class.

One special evening there was a loud knocking at my door. A little voice called out, "Are you home Mummy?" I hurried to open up the door, and there stood little Beven and Byron. Byron carries the largest bouquet of flowers I have ever seen. He enfolds me in his arms. We are all laughing amongst the flowers. I'm finally released from the bear hug and then Byron asks me if I would like to dine out with he and Beven.

"That would be lovely," I say, "Come in and sit down and I'll be with you in a few minutes." After I change into special clothes, I put these beautiful flowers into fresh water.

We go along to my old place of work, the Austral. There is a special dinner on and the food is delicious, really scrumptious. It seems ages since I have eaten out. Byron is very attentive and after the meal he pops the inevitable question that I have secretly been waiting for.

"Yes!" I reply, letting my emotions fly for the first time!

I really love this man; the years had stood the test of

time. Byron has changed, with his little boy and the loss of Colleen he has become a thoughtful, caring person. He has matured, he is a new person, that selfish guy has disappeared.

We marry on the 10th of December and the three of us go on a honeymoon together.

On our return George phones. "I have a surprise for you." George and John have prepared a welcome home surprise at the cafe. Their wives, Megan and Lucille, organize the party in place of a wedding reception which we didn't bother to have. It is such a lovely time together and the gifts keep piling up, we can't believe what they have done for us.

John gives a speech. "Now that my assistant is well and truly married and has her own business - Janine you are a well-established Accountant - don't let your husband get in the way, keep up the good work and be happy." Everyone laughs and claps their hands.

I am so happy with this man to whom I had given my heart when I was a teenager; my love over the years has not wavered, no matter how I tried to forget him.

I am young enough to wait a few more years to have children, I hope for two of my own and Byron is ready to wait awhile as well. This is so pleasing to me, he has really given up thinking of only what he wants, he has lost that selfish nature.

I thank God and know that my life with Byron will be pleasant, now that he is so understanding of my ambitions. And we will both continue to rear Bevan, as I have been his 'mum' for a long time.

About the Author

Joyce Cowen started to write stories at age eighty-nine and is still writing, aged ninety-three at the time of publication of this story. She also draws fantasy flowers, writes inspiring verses and produces cards featuring her drawings and verses.

Joyce's story is like Janine's in that during WWII the girls were left to work on farms, helping their parents to earn a living. Many married at a very young age and continued to live on farms.

Unlike Janine, she was not one of the girls who had a chance to leave home to further her education and follow her dreams. Joyce worked at home on the farm, while doing a sewing/drafting class in town, plus doing domestic work for a family, before leaving to marry Dave Cowen, who was working in timber at that time. She lives in north eastern NSW, Australia.